Message in
a Bottle

'**Message in a Bottle**'
An original concept by Elizabeth Dale
© Elizabeth Dale

Illustrated by Mona Meslier Menuau

Published by MAVERICK ARTS PUBLISHING LTD

Studio 11, City Business Centre, 6 Brighton Road,

Horsham, West Sussex, RH13 5BB

© Maverick Arts Publishing Limited November 2020

+44 (0)1403 256941

A CIP catalogue record for this book is available at the British Library.

ISBN 978-1-84886-725-3

Maverick
publishing
www.maverickbooks.co.uk

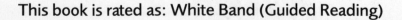

This book is rated as: White Band (Guided Reading)

Message in a Bottle

By Elizabeth Dale

Illustrated by
Mona Meslier
Menuau

Chapter 1

There was almost no one on the beach that evening. Jack loved the beach when it was empty, and so did Toby. Toby ran ahead, wagging his tail madly and sniffing all the interesting smells.

"Fetch, Toby!" Jack yelled, throwing a stick into the waves.

Whoops! Jack threw it further than he'd planned. Toby ran in, then quickly scurried back again as big waves rushed towards him. Jack laughed as the little dog just made it. And then he frowned. A bottle was lying next to Toby on the sand.

'More rubbish in the sea!' thought Jack crossly.

As he reached down to pick it up, Jack saw some paper in the bottle. He tipped it out expecting to find more rubbish. But it was a letter.

Hi, I'm Harry. Will you be my friend? Please message me back.

Jack looked around him. He wondered if someone had just thrown the bottle into the sea. But there was nobody about. Could this really be a message from someone a long way away? To him? All his life Jack had longed to find a message in a bottle. And now he had! Or was it a joke? Well, there was one way to find out.

He reached in his pocket and found a pencil and wrote on the note:

Hi, I'm Jack. I'd love to be your friend!

And then he put it in the bottle and threw it back into the sea.

Chapter 2

Jack was excited when he took Toby to the beach the following afternoon. He walked up and down the beach, but there was no bottle waiting for him, and no message.

At last, even Toby was tired. So Jack turned to go home. And then he saw it, lying on the sand. The bottle! With more paper inside! He cheered and took out the message, which read:

Hi Jack!

Great to hear from you. Tell me all about yourself. Do you like swimming and fishing? I've just been fishing and found the prettiest seahorse. Here's a picture. Tell me what you found today! What have you been doing?

Your friend, Harry.

Jack frowned. His life seemed so dull compared to Harry's. Imagine finding a seahorse! He'd never even seen one.

He wrote:

Hi Harry,

I didn't find anything today. I had a bad day. At school, we're doing a play. I went to the auditions, but then I wasn't sure, so I left. Now I wish I hadn't. I was just worried other kids would laugh at me. Why am I so scared of everything? I can't even swim because I'm scared of water. I wish I was braver. Your friend, Jack.

And then he shoved the note in the bottle, put the cork in, and threw it back in the waves. Immediately he regretted it. Harry wouldn't want to be his friend anymore! Not after reading what a coward he was.

Chapter 3

Jack didn't expect to get a reply the next day. He only went to the beach because Toby loved running there. But, amazingly, the bottle was washed up again!

Hi Jack, he read. I get scared of stuff too, like stormy weather and trying new things. You're so lucky to have a chance to be in a play. I'd love that. Why not try again? If kids laugh, it will be because they like you or they think you're funny. You show them! Harry.

Jack smiled. There were some more auditions tomorrow, after school. Probably not many people would go...

Hi Harry, he wrote. If you think I can do it, I'll try my best. But you must promise to try something new for me. Deal? Jack.

But at the auditions the next day, Jack almost lost his nerve. There were more children there than he'd imagined. He planned to escape again, but then he remembered his promise to Harry. Suddenly, Mr Jones called his name.

Slowly, Jack stood up. He was asked to play the part of someone who was terrified of ghosts. Well, he was scared alright! His voice trembled and his knees shook as he read the part. When he finished, everyone clapped.

"Well done, Jack," said Mr Jones. "You're in the play. You're brilliant!"

Jack *felt* brilliant! He ran down to the beach and eagerly read Harry's message saying how he'd tried something new – an underwater triple summersault.

Wicked! Jack wrote, And I'm in the play! Thanks to you!

The play rehearsals
went well. Jack described
them to Harry daily and
Harry told Jack about all the
new things he'd done because Jack
encouraged him.

As each day went by, they felt they knew each
other better than anyone, that they could write

messages about things they couldn't even mention to anybody else. They shared their fears and the same wacky sense of humour – and awful jokes!

Jack loved hearing about Harry's home, Shell Island, with its tame seabirds and empty, unspoiled beaches. And then one day, he had a brilliant idea. He wrote a quick note:

Let's meet! I'd love to see your beautiful beaches and maybe you could teach me to swim? And you could come and see me in my play?

Jack threw the message into the sea, then rushed home to ask his mum if they could go to Shell Island. Fortunately, she thought it was a great idea, and she arranged for a boat to take them on Saturday. Hooray!

Chapter 4

Friday was wild and stormy, but still Jack hurried to the beach to read Harry's reply. But there was no message. Maybe the bottle had smashed on a rock in the gale?

And then Jack recalled Harry writing that he was scared of stormy weather. Had he been too frightened to go out? He should help his pen-friend, the way Harry had helped him.

Jack rushed to the beach café, just as it was closing. The owner knew Jack well and gave him a used bottle and some paper. Jack wrote:

Don't worry, Harry, I will come to see you tomorrow. Meet me on your beach! Jack

And then he
threw it in the sea.
He hoped with all his heart
that tomorrow would be calmer!

The weather the next day was much better, so
the trip was on! Jack was so excited as he
stepped onto their boat, that he didn't notice
the bottle floating beside it. Or the note inside
it saying, No, Jack! Don't come!

The sea was blue, the sun was shining, and Jack grew more and more excited as they drew nearer to Shell Island. Soon he'd meet Harry! "Why are you so keen to visit here?" asked Tom, the boat-owner.

"Because my penpal lives here," said Jack.

Tom frowned. "That can't be right," he said.

"Why not?" said Jack. "We've been writing for months so he must live here."

"He can't do," said Tom. "Nobody lives on Shell Island. It's uninhabited."

Jack stared at him. He was wrong, he had to be!

Chapter 5

As soon as they arrived, Jack started to explore, but the island did seem to be totally deserted. The beach was empty. But then Jack recalled that Harry had said how he loved the empty beaches. Maybe his family kept it secret that they lived there?

"Are there any houses?" asked his mum.

"No," said Tom. "Only old ruins."

'Maybe Harry's family live in a cave,' thought Jack.

Jack checked the beach while his mum paddled in the sea. He ran along the cliffs, peering in all the caves, which looked just like the ones Harry had described. Harry couldn't have made it all up!

"Harry!" he called. "It's me, Jack. Where are you?"

But there was no reply. Jack started to worry. Maybe Harry hadn't got his message? But he was always on the beach... Where could he be?

Harry loved swimming, so maybe he was in the sea and hadn't seen them? Jack clambered along some rocks and gazed into the water.

"Harry?" he called.

"Yes?" Harry answered. Jack turned, smiling. Harry was there! In the sea, clinging onto a rock. "I told you not to come!" said Harry.

Jack frowned. "What?"

"I sent you a message," said Harry.

"I didn't get it," said Jack. " I'm sorry. Why?"

"Because this spoils everything," Harry said.

Jack stared at him. "Why?" he said. "I don't understand."

"Because now you know the truth about me," said Harry. And he swung his tail onto the rocks.

Jack stared at him, stunned.
"You're... a... mermaid!" he whispered.

"No, I'm a merboy!" Harry said crossly.

"Of course. I'm sorry! Wow! Wow! WOW! This is amazing!" Jack said.

"You mean... you don't mind?" asked Harry, anxiously. "I was sure you would."

"What? No way!" Jack cried. "I didn't even know merboys existed! I think it's brilliant!"

"So... you still wish to be my friend?" Harry asked.

"More than ever!" Jack grinned. "You can teach me all about your world. And with you beside me, I'm sure I could brave the sea and learn to swim. We're going to have such fun together!"

Harry smiled at him. "We are. Who'd have thought that my message in a bottle could lead me to the best friend ever!"

The End

Book Bands for Guided Reading

The Institute of Education book banding system is a scale of colours that reflects the various levels of reading difficulty. The bands are assigned by taking into account the content, the language style, the layout and phonics. Word, phrase and sentence level work is also taken into consideration.

Maverick Early Readers are a bright, attractive range of books covering the pink to white bands. All of these books have been book banded for guided reading to the industry standard and edited by a leading educational consultant.

Pink

Red

Yellow

Blue

Green

Orange

Turquoise

Purple

Gold

White

To view the whole Maverick Readers scheme, visit our website at

www.maverickearlyreaders.com

Or scan the QR code above to view our scheme instantly!